Hook™

P

TH

Adapted from a screenplay by
Jim V. Hart and Malia Scotch Marmo

From a screen story by
Jim V. Hart & Nick Castle

Illustrated by Mones

Random House New York

 Published in the United States by Random House, Inc., New York, and simultaneously in Canada by Random House of Canada Limited, Toronto. Library of Congress Catalog Card Number: 91-62089 ISBN: 0-679-82702-1

Manufactured in the United States of America 10 9 8 7 6 5 4 3 2

Kerplunk! A large clamshell rose from the sea and crashed onto the shores of the faraway Neverland. Out stepped Peter Banning, a businessman from New York City.

"W-w-where am I? What in the world...?" he uttered in total confusion.

"Where *are* you? You're finally home in Neverland, with the Lost Boys—the boys who never want to grow up," said a small fluttering faerie named Tinkerbell. "And you're Peter Pan, the boys' leader. Don't you remember *anything*?"

All Peter could remember was that he and his family had been visiting his wife's grandmother, Wendy, in London... and while he was attending a formal dinner party, his two kids had been kidnapped... and then a faerie had come along and said she would help him get them back!

"Boys! Boys! It's Pan! He's back!" shouted Tink as she flew furiously around the Nevertree, the tree village of the Lost Boys. She pounded on doors and dumped Lost Boys off hammocks.

"Pan! Pan!" yelled the boys as they shoved one another and tried to get a better view.

"Hey, he's too old and fat to be Pan," shouted Ace, one of the boys. "And look at that belly! He must be at *least* forty! Sure doesn't look like the Pan *I* knew!"

But it *was* the Pan he had known. Pan had just grown up—the one thing he was never supposed to do! And the only reason he was here was to get his kids back from the evil Captain Hook.

"AH-AH—AH-AHHHH!" A deafening crowing sound suddenly rang out over Neverland, and Rufio, the current leader of the Lost Boys, appeared atop a speeding windcoaster, sword in hand.

"Hey, you, be careful there!" yelled Peter. "You shouldn't play with swords. Isn't anyone in charge? Aren't there any grownups around here?"

That did it! *No one* mentions grownups in Neverland and gets away with it. Peter Pan or not, this grownup had to be stopped. In an instant, the boys readied themselves for all-out war.

"All grownups are pirates. We hate pirates. Get him!" they yelled in chorus and began swooping at Peter from all sides—on skateboards, on skates, circling him, doing figure eights. There was no escaping now!

"Stop! Stop!" yelled Tinkerbell. "He's your captain! Believe me! He's just forgotten. He needs you to help him get his children back, and you need him!"

"Ha! Some captain!" yelled Rufio as he managed to corner Peter and shove him up against a fence. "Okay, man. If you're really Pan, you've gotta prove it. Pan could fly, fight, and crow. Can ya fly? Can ya fight? Can ya crow? Huh?"

Peter thought only birds crowed, but he figured he'd take a try at it, along with fighting. After all, it seemed his kids' lives—and his own—depended on it. As for flying—he'd leave that for later!

So Ace handed him a sword, but the weight made him teeter sideways! And as for his crow—it was hardly more than a feeble "coo"!

"What did I say!" cried Rufio triumphantly as he plugged his ears. "You *still* think this is Pan?" he asked, turning to Tinkerbell.

“Of *course* this is Pan,” said Tink, throwing her hands in the air. “Trust me. He needs all of you more than ever. He needs to fight Hook, and it’s up to *us* to get him in shape. Get out the running shoes, Thud Butt. Wind up the stopwatch. We’re going to bring back the Pan we knew.”

And so the Lost Boys started Pan on a daily routine: jogging before breakfast, pull-ups and leg lifts—a complete aerobic workout.

“Enough! Enough!” gasped Peter after several hours. “How is *this* going to help me get my kids back?”

"Trust me," said Tink again. "*This* will make the boys believe, Hook believe, and most important—it will make *you* believe that you are who you are—PAN. And now you *must* fly."

With that, Thud Butt had an idea. The Lost Boys built a giant replica of Thud Butt's slingshot—big enough for Peter to sit in! And several boys rigged up a net—big enough for Peter to land in!

Once Peter was strapped into the slingshot, the Lost Boys lined up and pulled... pulled... ever so slowly. And with every step backward, the elastic band stretched a little more....

"Think a happy thought—any happy thought. With that, and a little faerie dust, you can *flyyyy*—straight off this cliff!" said Tink.

So Peter tried. He tried with all his might, but when Tink said "cotton candy," he thought "cavities." When she said "snow," he thought "slush," and when she said "summer," he thought "mosquitoes"! Hardly happy thoughts!

So when Rufio cut the rope that had been holding the slingshot taut, Peter went sailing up, up—far into the sky. But he just as quickly came down, down—straight into the giant net!

"I need to eat, build up strength," said Peter as he limped to a place at the Lost Boys' table.

"Time for Neverfood!" responded Ace as he placed a large steaming platter before Peter. But when the steam cleared away, what did Peter see on his plate? Nothing!

"Hey, what's the big idea?" Peter asked angrily. He looked down the table and saw boy after boy ravenously devouring...NOTHING!

"You remember this game, don't you, Peter?" said Tink, smiling and darting away from some imaginary food being flung across the table. "You used to love it! In fact, you invented it!"

It was bad enough that there was no food at this meal, but when Rufio finished eating and shoved his tray across the table and hit Peter in the chest with it, that was *enough*.

"You, you, you little..." began a red-faced Peter as he slowly rose from the table.

"Yeah? What? Say it, old geezer. Say it!" challenged Rufio with a mocking smirk on his face.

"You are a badly raised child!" said Peter.

"Huh?" said Thud Butt. "*Badly raised child? Badly raised child?* This sure ain't the Peter Pan *we* knew."

Peter was getting really mad now. "You... you... crude, rude bag of pre-chewed food!"

At this, the boys exploded with excitement. "Bangerang, Peter!" they yelled in chorus.

And Rufio hurled a great plate of imaginary food right at Peter. But as it hit, the food became real! Hungry Peter eagerly gobbled it up. Then, with renewed energy, he hurled a plate back at Rufio. *Splat!*—turkey and stuffing landed all over Rufio's face!

With excitement the boys lined up around Peter and started yelling, "You're doing it, Peter! You're doing it!"

"Doing *what?*" asked Peter. "Eating?"

"No, silly. Playing! Like us! Like a kid… like *Peter Pan!*" they all said at once.

Tink beamed and did several very fine figure eights in the air.

Suddenly, full of rage, Rufio picked up two heavy coconuts. He eyed Peter coldly and loaded up a shot at Peter's head.

"Hey, Peter, watch it!" yelled Ace as another boy tossed Peter a sword. Swiftly catching it and spinning around, Peter gracefully sliced *both* coconuts in perfect halves.

As everything came to a rapid halt, a loud gasp was heard. It came from Peter. A new but familiar feeling of fun was charging through him. Maybe what Tink said was true... maybe he really *was* Pan, and if he could just keep having fun, she said... like a kid...

The boys all lined up around Peter with enormous hope and admiration in their eyes.

Now that Peter had remembered how to have fun and play, surely he would remember how to fight, to fly, and to crow. . . and once he could do that—A-A-A-AHHHHHHHHH!—why, he could do nearly anything! He could even rescue his children from the evil Captain Hook!